PRAISE ~~FOR HURRICANE~~

MW00617517

"Hurricane Trinity is a gorgeous storm of tenderness, surprise, and devastation."

Meagan Lucas, author of *Songbirds and Stray Dogs* and *Here in the Dark*, Editor in Chief of Reckon Review

"Nick Gardner writes with crushing and pain embracing honesty. With eloquence, Hurricane Trinity is a stunning novella about questioning and yet embracing life with newfound hope. Weather also plays a crucial role, as it does daily now. It becomes a central metaphor, and is essentially a central forte. The work is wistful, playful, and liminal, and proves to be much larger than the sum of its parts. With his idiosyncratic magic, Gardner transforms and uplifts the most mundane spaces into shimmering sites of the uncanny."

Robert Vaughan, author of *ASKEW*, Editor in Chief of Bending Genres

"Nick Rees Gardner's Hurricane Trinity tells of depression, climate grief, and family struggles, all against the backdrop of a declining Gulf Coast town threatened by ocean rise and devastating storms. Gardner peers into the tumultuous inner world of Devin, a mother haunted by visions of the future, and shows her inner world reflected by the world at large.

Hurricane Trinity is spare and elegant, as the novella form demands, and also large in scope and ambition, exploring the questions of our time. I read this brilliant work in a single sitting."

Lawrence Coates, author of *Camp Olvido*

HURRICANE TRINITY

A NOVELLA
BY NICK REES GARDNER

I.

Devin wants to disappear, but vanishing seems like a cop-out, or maybe she is just afraid. She reads about Edna Pontellier walking out into the ocean and it scares her how tempted she is by this liberation in death. She knows it doesn't have to be like that. There must be some balance between the overwhelm of love and its burden.

She holds hands with her children, mourning the dead hermit crab, its body munched on by sea foam. She understands the impossibility of leaving them behind. Just as the characters from stories stick with her, Devin knows that the shape of missing her will always float in her children's minds long after she is gone. Every year, the Gulf inches closer to their home, the hurricanes swing with more power, and Devin wonders if the world will outlast them or if they will outlast the world. But, as long as they can share moments like this, it isn't hopeless.

As they stand in the sand of Sunport Beach, she squeezes her children and feels full. Towhead Layla on her left, unabashed in six-year-old chunkiness, who wants nothing more than to panda-bear onto Devin's ankle and be dragged around the floor while Devin sets the table or gathers up the trash. On her right, eight-year-old Andrew inspires Devin with his stillness, his ability to sit quietly on the front porch for hours deep in thought. There is a certain depth in his gaze. He is a mystery, and she can only ever access fragments of what goes on beneath his curls. This family is her stable center while the world rushes around them like a maniac.

Before the hermit crab's funeral was the homicide. That morning, when Devin looked through the kitchen window, she saw Andrew on the back patio about to smash the shell with a brick. She burst into tears, thinking that maybe he had entered into some larval stage of serial killer. Her throat caught around a ball of doubt about where she went wrong. Genetic or socialized, she is complicit in all her son's actions. She watched as he held the brick above the crab. He hesitated before dropping it. Crunch.

In truth, Andrew only wanted to see the crustacean naked. That was why he cleaned out an old perfume bottle: in hopes that the crab would make the transparent chamber its new home. But the crab would have to be evicted first. At eight years old, Andrew didn't understand the physics of the situation. He learned the fragility of life when he brought the brick down on the animal's abdomen, wound deep in its Fibonacci spiral, and as his mother came through the door ready to both choke and cling to her beautiful, troubled son, he ran to her in tears begging for forgiveness. He told her everything because she is intermediary to all those pieces of the universe which he can't yet access. And she, then, was only grateful that her son wasn't lost, and they gathered the pieces of both shell and crab body, and they gathered Andrew's sister Layla in order to hold a proper funeral service on the shore.

On the beach they now stand, three in a row, mother in the middle holding a small wooden box filled with crushed remains. The waves, whipped up by an imminent rain, froth at their tips and slap at the toes of the mourners who don't back off, only take another step deeper, the tide pulling at their ankles, then their calves. Devin says, Andrew, would you like to say some words? And Andrew says, Saltine crackers, albatross, antidisestablishmentarianism. Some words.

He is deadpan. He looks up proudly at his mother, her hair a dark storm in the wind, pale face, sunless but smiling, a slim line of white scar along her cheek. Andrew cracks a grin as well, the crab already having passed from memory to ceremony and, finally, to humor in his mind. Layla plugs her thumb into her mouth, clutches her mother's dress with her free hand. Devin smiles at each child because it is not the right time to kiss them.

Devin says, To crab. The crabbiest of all the crabs! And she casts the body, the crushed shell in its tiny wooden box, at the ceaseless surf.

The beauty of homeschool is that Andrew has time to explore the world with his friends. He stands on the beach in the inhale of mid-spring, licked by the drops of ocean spray, playing Bombs Away with Kiley and Gerry. Kiley and Gerry are the only twins Andrew knows and the only girls he has met who can outthrow, outswim, and outrun him. He wouldn't consider himself athletic though. Not really. Gerry hurls her stone-bomb so far it disappears into a wave. Andrew pulls a smooth rock from his pocket, crouches, and, with his whole body, underhands it skyward. He yells, Watch out! And the three children scream and scramble while the rock seems to float for eons in the salt air, the bright sun and breeze. Then it finally plummets with a subtle plunk on the sand. The children stand like compass points around the rock's center, the Gulf to the south, taking one last look over the sheer everything before turning back home.

Andrew lives across the highway from the ocean next to the vacation rental condos of the Sunset Villas, which once were packed with visitors all season long, but now sit empty as the summer blazes in. Hurricane season is coming. Flanking the house on either side like siege towers are two hotels in constant states of construction and, instead of a front yard, there is a vacant parking lot with yellow grass poking through its seams. Andrew's mother can sit on the porch and look over the lot across the highway and watch the speck of distant Andrew on the beach. Now that he is eight, he is allowed to cross the highway, playing by the ocean without an adult by his side. He isn't allowed to enter the water unless his mother is there. But that isn't really a temptation. There is something terrible in the waves. He wants to be close to the water but doesn't want it to touch him.

Cars whoosh by on four lanes, making Andrew's mom, lazing on the front porch with her novel, a choppy blur. She says she always watches over their adventures on the beach, but Andrew knows his mom's books disappear the world around her. She perches there as only the symbol of a sentinel, her eyes turned inward where there is no beach, no house, no daughter or son. When traffic slows, blurs become individual cars and trucks rumbling in place at their red light, and Andrew and the twins clutch hands to run barefoot across the sand-blown and sun-rubbery asphalt up the path back home.

Dad gets back from work in the late afternoon and emerges from his bedroom moments later in his swim trunks, towel tucked under his arm. They go swimming in the Sunset Villas' pool. Andrew sometimes wonders why they can't walk in the front entrance, why they creep around the stucco walls to the gate where his dad tiptoes up, reaches over, and unhooks the catch from inside the fence, but the pool makes Andrew forget to ask. The pale green water used to be filled with children and adults of all ages from the early spring to late fall, but these last couple years it has been mostly empty. Andrew never knew his father's uncle, just that, according to Andrew's dad, the land where the Sunset Villas now stand was once his uncle's land, so the pool is basically theirs. Of course, there have been times when Andrew's dad made them leave the pool and book it to the exit, which makes Andrew wonder who really rules over this space. But before he can turn his doubt into words, his dad dives. Andrew teeters on the edge until Kiley swipes her arm along the surface, pushing a pool-sized wave that hits Andrew's stomach and he, losing his hesitance, jumps and balls up in the air to splash the twins back.

They play Marco Polo in the shallow end while a couple other kids, quiet, sour-faced brothers just a bit older, cling to the walls in the deeper water. Their grandma sits with a newspaper that keeps wrinkling itself in the breeze. She scowls over the sports section. These other children come and go. These vacationers never become friends with Andrew, just distant neighbors from another state, another world. The twins are his friends because they know the freedom of the empty beach, the rules and secrets of the Villas, the vacant lot. The visitors always watch Andrew and his family as if they might bite, strays leftover in a place where no one is meant to live.

Andrew, his sister, and the twins take turns swimming over to Andrew's dad and climbing onto the ledge of his shoulders to dive back into the water. Andrew splashes a can opener a couple feet from Layla, sending a boy-sized tsunami over her head, and of course she begins sobbing. One of the sour-faced brothers swims over to Andrew's father and begins to climb up, and the grandmother launches from her seat saying, Nicky! No! Don't touch that man! Stay away!

Nicky's face twists up terrified and he doesn't move, but Andrew's dad only nods to Andrew and the twins and moonwalks to the shallow end, hoists a silenced but still teary-eyed Layla up and sack-of-potatoes her over his shoulder. The water beaded on his tattoos sparkles in the sunlight. He says, It's time to go kiddos. Then, more loudly, We don't want to upset anyone.

He nods to Andrew, who follows, dripping out of the water and leaves footprints on his way along the cement. The grandmother mumbles in their wake and the sour-faced boys tread water grumpily.

Back at the house, Layla holes up in the kitchen drawing pictures while Andrew and the twins don't change out of their swimsuits but suck on popsicles on the front porch waiting for the girls' moms to pick them up and take them half an hour inland to their home. Kiley says, Guess what? Mom says we're going to school this year. Like real school. Mom says it will be *conducive* to our education to learn more social skills.

The school year is ending and then more tourists will come. The beaches will be lightly peppered with sunbathers, the Villas bouncing with pop songs and college students, anyone too broke for the finer shores yet unravaged by rising oceans, the vacation cabanas and knick-knack shops. But it will still mean less pool time for Andrew, a hot sun that will keep him inside and bored much of the day. He says, What's *conducive*?

Gerry says, It's just something that you get at real school. You wouldn't understand.

Andrew says, But what about our field trips? We'll still go to the zoo and stuff together. Or the museum.

Not on school days, says Kiley, 'cause we'll be in real school. We'll go on field trips on the bus with the other kids.

Andrew pictures the twins lining up at the museum, a string of partners, and a teacher leading their way while Andrew holds his mom's hand. He doesn't like the strictness of the lines of students, the way the teachers herd the kids, telling them to catch up while Andrew and Layla are only reigned in when they wander out of their mom's sight. And his mom whispers the details of each painting, each sculpture, reads excerpts of history from the museum's pamphlets. The harsh structure of school and school kids. How could anyone want that? But then, he also remembers the way the kids punch one another's arms or laughed together while Andrew, Mom, and Layla eat their quiet lunch at the Orh O'Keefe.

Kiley and Gerry's moms pull up in a silver minivan. They roll down the windows, sniff the air like there's something foul in it. The sunset hangs over the empty parking lot, and the twins hop from the deck, run to the van, their mothers, their school, their inland life. Andrew doesn't get up, only waves goodbye as his mom comes out, talks through the rolled down window, smiling away as the day ends.

Night comes.

Devin blames it on the heat when she begins to have dreams where her teeth fall out. Also, sometimes throughout the day, bending over her little Andrew and circling the series of dots on his worksheet to show him how math is only numbers, and how numbers stand for things, she sees visions of him as a man with a gun in his hand and dead bodies all around. Or she imagines pulling up his sleeve and staring into the constellations of track marks on his hairy adult arm. She wants to throw him on the ground and pummel every possible future evil out of him. Should she even be a mother if this is the kind of future she predicts? She chokes herself with these thoughts that come so suddenly out of nowhere. She feels sick. She has to tell him—gulping her sobs back into herself—that math is over for the day, go play. He dumps his bucket of Legos on the living room floor while she locks herself in the bathroom, sits down on the edge of the tub, and cries.

Think. She has to think.

It is something about the weather, record highs. The heat presses her further into the earth while also covering her mouth, stifling her breath, helpless like the thirteen-year-old girl who was kidnapped, choked on her own sock, and left in Boca Raton to rot. The world is more than half horrible, the rest dangerous. Yes, the globe grows unnaturally warmer every year, and especially so in Sunport, Alabama. This is nature's signal that the coming summer will be another downer, and she gropes for something solid to cling to. When she looks back, she can't remember how long this decline has been going on. Probably before she was born, but it seems that it has been only recently that she became aware enough to be sad about it. The only time she feels sane is when she buries herself deep in a book, but she can hardly pay attention to books anymore. Devin lies back, scans a sentence ten, twenty times, and watches Layla and Andrew as they cross the highway, trying to trust them not to get hit by a car or get murdered. They are too far away for her to sprint over and save. But she must give them at least a slight amount of distance, allow them some trust even though her heart flutters. Andrew clutches Layla's hand. They look at each other and grin before crossing. This is how she knows her children will lead miserable lives, because Devin is too hot, too tired to protect them.

Mornings come on like hangovers even though she quit drinking years ago. She wakes in a sour mood, grunts, rolls over to punch the snooze button on her phone, then is woken up immediately by her second alarm. She snoozes again and, again, her phone goes off, immediately. Somehow, though, she finds she has overslept by an hour. She knows what is going on, all these telltale signs of depression, but it can't be mental illness, just doldrums that come and go, a response to a dire world. Depression isn't in her family. She googles homeopathic and self-care methods, reads articles on her phone while she sits on the porch. Sometimes, it is just mind over matter. Sometimes, there is so much to worry about in the world that it makes her feel like slumping through the floor. She deletes the news apps from her phone so she doesn't have to deal with global dread. It is a start.

Her husband, Ely, eats breakfast with the kids that morning. Avocado toast, tomatoes, and a fruit salad. He has a plate made up for her. She manages to smile through the extravagant meal and even finds the strength to kiss Ely and tell him she loves him before he slings his backpack over his shoulder and heads out the door. He turns back, says, Everything alright, honey? Ely can always sense when something is off.

I'm fine, she says. Just might be coming down with something.

Should I stay home?

Devin says, No. Go.

Layla is latched onto her ankle this whole time. Devin feels the urge to shake her leg and imagines Layla's body losing its grip and flying off into a wall or bookshelf, snapping the wood and bones. What a horrible thing to think. Devin feels the pressure building, an ocean wishing to break from her tear ducts. The waves crash at the beach, louder and louder. A storm curls around the horizon.

Layla says in a whiney voice, Mom, do we have to do school today? Why can't we just play?

Devin sighs, limps her ball-and-chain of Layla to the couch, and crashes down. From the kitchen table, Andrew says, Yeah, I'm already ahead on math.

The point of homeschooling was to give the children more, but what if Devin has nothing more to give? She used to build sculptures, to draw and paint. She wanted to pass this manner of self-expression and release down to her children, but there is no time for that anymore. Her hand finds its way to her cheek, the white scar that runs along it, a gift from those freer days, from a man much less nurturing than Ely, more furious and careless. This scar is a symbol of the end of that journey, when she changed majors from art to education. And with this change she has been able to teach her children first hand. She tries not to think of it as sacrificing art for kids, but her selfish ego knows that is exactly what she has done, that she would have been better off alone.

In the corner next to the TV is her final art project, sculpted just before she changed majors, the ruins of an industrial arch with iron flowers welded to it. All that scrap metal from the Rust Belt. She, at once, misses her home in Ohio and hates it. She misses and hates the freedom she used to have, the sleeping off hangovers, the waking up with strangers, and the balling up in her bed in the morning alone to, every once in a while, cry over missing someone. She could have been a great artist, or maybe never made it. She wants her children to have choices, options. She wants to try harder.

The next morning, Devin wakes up booger-eyed at 5:30 a.m. to take the kids on the hour trip along the coast to the seashell beach. Devin drives and thinks of Ely, still asleep. Strange to be awake before him. There is pride in giving him a morning off, in slipping from under the covers, waking the kids, and then showering quickly. In being the one to kiss Ely's cheek rather than he hers, and say, See you this afternoon, while he grunts and rolls over. She loads the van with bags and buckets in the dawn-quiet dark, air chilled just enough to make any skin it touches feel alive. She keeps the window cracked as they hush along the highway past

Pensacola, the salt smell and whip of air is alive all around them.

At their secret shore, a stretch of sand between a large hotel and the private beach belonging to a series of abandoned condos, they plant a chair in the sand as a beacon and begin their search. Devin brings her Florida Seashells book and, right off the bat, she spots a pristine Fighting Conch. They lay the first footsteps of the day along the beach, the water receding as the moon releases its pull. Layla finds Scotch Bonnets, begins to walk ahead plucking one shell after another. She turns, realizes she is so wonderfully far from her mother and brother, then runs back to them, cupped hands brimming with this strange ocean bounty. This is a teaching moment. Devin tells the children about Cowries, how they are currency and also worn as jewelry. She speaks of wampum used by indigenous people on the East Coast. They walk the lonely beach for hundreds of feet or for miles, towering hotels and resorts only specters in the blurry morning distance. Andrew picks up a battered Cockle and asks what he could buy with it and Devin says, How about you trade it to me for a sandwich? Andrew draws back and heaves the pitted shell into the wake. Says, But I'll get the sandwich anyway.

Andrew drags behind and Layla plows ahead. Vacant houses hem the sand, mostly wrecked by the hurricane waves that have swelled higher and higher with each storm and each year of melting ice caps. They pass a set of six snapped-off wooden poles that once stilted a house, now swept away to the submarine netherworld. Nobody lives in the houses that are left since they became uninsurable, since there are nicer beaches less storm-torn. The windows and sliding doors of the vacation homes are missing, not even boarded-over. Their porches are twisted wrecks or they are completely gone. Their paint has faded from the scraping of wind and sand. The salt air corrodes the metal joists and pipes. Large driftwood trees lie in the shape of dead whale shadows as the sun rises. The waves keep crashing, crashing, crashing.

There is an instant that Devin loves, right before a wave turns over and falls, when it has risen and floats toward her, overtaking itself silently. A calm before the splash, yes, but also a sense of growing.

Ever since Ely convinced Devin to move to Sunport, April has been his favorite month. The sun doesn't throb like in July or August. The semester doesn't end until May, and he will have to teach summer classes at the community college anyway, but he eases up his students' workload, grades with a laxer curve. As the days continue to lengthen, he feels freer. This year, he is on the hiring committee and the English Department is struggling to find faculty who want to teach four sections per semester at poverty-level wages without insurance. The adjunct struggle is real. A real pain in Ely's ass. He tries to publish to prove his worth, attends conferences and meetings, as if that will make him relevant. But more and more, the job is all about struggling for engagement and getting student evals. Plus, the bureaucracy makes him sick. So, he has learned to separate the fullness of life from the stagnation that is work. Especially at the end of term.

Ely speeds on his way home to his family every night, cooks dinner or eats what Devin has cooked. Sometimes, he orders pizza and picks it up on the 40-minute commute. He likes to bake—lasagnas, pies, coffee cake—while Devin prefers to never turn the oven dial, only messes with a series of pots and pans, a wok, maybe, on the range. Ely remembers dating Devin in college. He was cooking a meal for her birthday in her studio apartment, chopping onions with eyes streaming as the oven preheated. And then the smell of burnt plastic. Smoke billowed from the oven as he opened the door to melted cutting boards and piping hot pots and pans. She told him she never turned the oven on. She kissed him. The oven became the butt of a series of jokes between them, then evolved into only a grin whenever he touched the knob.

Tonight, he will bake shells and cheese, red sauce in a pan, an old family recipe. A Midwestern magic trick of sorts where he will turn $5 worth of ingredients into a feast with distinct thrifty pride. Devin is out on a run. Running was his suggestion. Fresh air, time away from the kids in the evenings. She deserves it, he thinks, after spending the entire day at home. You can love your children so much and still be overwhelmed by them. Devin is a fantastic runner with a gait like a suspended antelope, legs paddling in the hangtime between touchdown. Maybe it would help with the recent lethargy that she calls her Summertime Sadness, after the song. She will not admit to depression and won't see a counselor. But even healthy people run. It makes sense. Better diet, better physique. She tells him, It's just a lack of motion. A body in motion stays in motion, and I haven't been moving much at all.

Ely says, Yes. Momentum.

Momentum, Devin repeats as she loops the bunny ears on her Asics, lifts her knees high, then takes off out the door.

Ely thinks of momentum as he tries to squeeze in grading a paper while the shells bake. Feminist theory tears chunks out of the The Great American Novel. For Ely, the entire point of teaching is when he gets that one paper with a fuck-the-man attitude behind it. He loves a punk-ass rebellious student. He loves to see that passion, that anger at the way things are and that desire to change. As much as it pisses him off, he loves watching the careful stares of the Sunset Villas vacationers when he strips his shirt to reveal his torso roped in tattoos, stick and pokes from the Cleveland Heights days and Deadhead nods from his pothead college years. He likes to say ain't in front of his more uppity colleagues and wear hoodies when he teaches class, to fuck propriety. There is a way people twist their lips that floors him, lets him know he has made an impact. At the Villas, he smiled for weeks after he watched the crowd gathered around the wadded-up brownie he once left like a turd by the pool. But now, the Villas' vacationers are sparse, walled off from the poverty-flecked ghost town around them and all his attempts at disrupting their comfort have been for nothing.

It only took a series of storms, large waves and cuts in federal aid to scare off the upper-middle-classes and their snowbird elders.

The timer beeps and he gets up to shut it off. Checks the shells, sets another five minutes.

Layla wiggles her hips in the kitchen doorway for a moment, then runs over and latches onto his leg. She says, Can I help, Daddy?

He tells her there is nothing really to be done. But of course, if she wants to be involved, she should be, so he says, But you could do the salad?

He pulls tomatoes from the fridge along with the lettuce, carrots, and he chops and throws them into the bowl that Layla wildly tosses with salad tongs, vegetable pieces jettisoned to the floor.

Layla says, Why does Mommy run at night?

It makes her hungry for dinner, Ely says.

But why does she take so many naps during the day?

Ely doesn't have an answer ready. He didn't know about naps. Of course, naps are normal. But just what do the children do while Devin is sleeping? Probably not schoolwork.

He says, How about this? What do red vegetables have on the ends of their feet?

What? Says Layla.

TomaTOES, he says.

Layla grins kindly. She sees it as a challenge. She says, Okay, but what does lettuce have on its fingers?

What? says Ely.

They wear rings made out of seaweed and diamonds that are like Jell-O. Or, I mean... popsicles! She laughs through her nose, spilling more salad on the floor.

Ely is a good man, and sometimes this makes Devin feel worse about herself. She cries almost daily now. She wants to keep the world from her children, bury its grief deep. The sadness sprawls her face-first on the couch while Layla reads to herself and Andrew draws his still-lifes at the kitchen table. She has cut herself off from the outside world, and so it is a sourceless sadness, originating from nothing, meaning nothing. Then she recovers and moves herself from the couch to the kitchen to cook or clean. Or she is able to pick up a book and read *Charlotte's Web* to a rapt Layla until Ely gets home. Devin lets the tears soak the cushion and then sleeps while the cushion dries itself. This isn't like the familiar fatigue she knows, the one that came from all-night study sessions in college. Her body has all the energy it needs, but none of the desire.

She yanks on her running pants, stretches her sports bra over her body, studies her midriff where the weight is bunched like dough with little integrity. She squeezes the flesh around her belly button and makes it talk: *You wouldn't be getting fat now, would you?* Oh, me? No. She says. No. *You wouldn't be lying now?* says her belly. Ely is gone and she walks out of the bathroom, timbers onto her bed. She isn't sleeping, but her brain is empty. She isn't dead, not anything right now. The bed is almost as comfortable as being held.

The next day, she falls asleep on the couch around noon and wakes up in the evening. She feels Ely's body sitting at her feet, his hands massaging her soles. She wonders why he has come home early. Then she notices the twilit windows, the orange of sunset that holds the room in long shadows. She has been asleep all day. Where have the kids been?

Ely says, Babe, can I get you anything?

She wants to scratch him, to grasp at his face with her nails and ruin it. She holds this violence back. She says, Honey. But she can't complete the sentence. Her head expands like a water balloon filled with an ocean of tears. She says, I need to go for a run.

He says, Okay, but then can we talk?

She runs. She agrees with Ely that, yes, maybe it is this feeling of being trapped in the house that brings her down. Exercise improves mental health. She tried yoga first, but most days never made it out of Shavasana. She tried calisthenics, jumping jacks with the kids who mostly just fell over in awkward poses and mocked her or the activity itself. So it was back to running. Running is as easy as lacing up your shoes and stepping through the door. There is fresh air. The noise of the world ranges all around. To provide motivation, she asks Ely to mark her runs on the calendar, to call to let her know he is on his way home. It's time to get ready.

While she runs, the city grays around her into night. Ely, back at home, grades English comp papers from his class at the Community College and she can easily block him, their entire life together, out of her mind. She pushes her runs later as days grow longer. As July peaks, she runs while her children are in bed dreaming their own magic and terror. At night there are fewer people out in Sunport Beach. At this time the rest of her family is occupied and doesn't presently need her. She kicks off of the asphalt in a rhythm all her own, parses through memories, dreams of cocktails on the porch with friends, of riding bikes passively from party to party like in Columbus when she was in school and she slept with boys and abandoned them. A life with nothing to hang over her and a net beneath to catch her. Enough hope in front of her to perform miracles, to be beaten and shrug it off. As she runs, her past haunts her and draws her in, but then she is released.

The anatomy of the jog begins with a skin of dread and failure. She ludicrously believes, for example, that Ely is sleeping with one of his students. Devin knows she isn't satisfying as a partner. She is often too tired for sex. Ely doesn't push her, which most likely means he doesn't want her like he used to, or that he gets what he wants from somewhere else. Devin thinks of the time back in April when she glanced at a student paper that Ely was grading and saw that Ely had written in the margin, "Love!" It was a "Love!" that went beyond a mere compliment. It was the same

"Love!," in fact, that he had scribbled in the margin of a bad poem she had written him back when they first started dating. It is a "Love!" that's shared between strangers who want more, want that "Love!" intimacy of body against body. Devin knows this and doesn't hate him. She doesn't have the facts to confront him. It doesn't take much to send Devin's mind straight to perplexity.

Then she thinks about the musculature: what if her own bouts of tears chase her children away from her? What if they write tell-all books about the struggles of growing up with a depressive mother? How their mother's sadness and worry has cheated them out of the innocence of childhood that their friends knew? What if she has robbed them of important life experience? What if they wrote about how their father always made all the meals, always took care of them while their mother only slept?

As Devin breathes deeper, picks up her pace, her brain starves itself of oxygen, shuts off these problems. She cuts through, now, to the guts of herself, these fond memories of the end of high school, the beginning of college. And finally, these guts give way to the bare bones, and it is as if she has caught herself daydreaming through a conversation, has been shocked back to reality with a laugh. It is good to feel her body. Each clenched fist, the give of cartilage, real physical soreness. She can focus on the pain of the body rather than the pain of the mind. The further she goes, the more her thoughts quiet and cool.

By the middle of summer, Andrew has had enough of homeschool. He is alone with his sleepy mother all week long and then goes to Kiley and Gerry's on the weekend. They hardly ever even come to his house anymore. Kiley and Gerry have been filling him in. There are hundreds of people at school, whole rooms filled with students who all want to be your friend. Teachers will jump to explain every question he has. If he can convince his parents to send him to school, he will see the twins every day, between classes, whispering from desk to desk. Gerry says that there are science classes where you can cut open worms with a knife and look at their insides.

Andrew says, They do that for school?

Kiley says, And even frogs!

At home, his mom is always tired and Andrew wonders if maybe he has been so much of a burden that his very existence is what wears her down. He wonders if there is a point where his questions become too much. She asks him if he understands a word problem and he says yes, even though he has no idea how many cookies Sandy can make with three bags of flour. His mom says, Good, honey. I'm going to go lie down for a minute.

Is his mother sick?

He asks if he can read to her while she rests, but she tells him not now and shuts the bedroom door. He hears the lock turn. He wonders if she knows of his betrayal, his desire for another teacher.

He waits til Sunday and calls a house meeting. Mom next to Dad on the couch, Layla cross-legged on the ground with a scowl.

He decides he will ease them into it. He paces in front of the coffee table, hands clutched behind his back. He says, Mom and Dad, I first want to say that Kiley and Gerry both would be in my class at school. If I went. And if I go to school, it will give you more time to focus on Layla's education.

Layla grins up at him.

Andrew says, Finally, I believe it would be more conducive to my social education to go to school. I need to understand people my age better.

Conducive? His mom says, Where do you get a word like conducive?

I just know it, alright?

Well what does it mean? Do you know what it means?

Andrew says, Favorable to, aiding a certain outcome. I know how to use the dictionary, Mom.

His dad cuts in, Andrew. Your mother and I respect your position, but this is something we need to discuss. It is not your decision alone. We will certainly take these points under consideration.

Andrew says he understands, but his mom begins to cry, and his dad only hugs her, says, It's fine honey.

His mom says, But, of course it's fine. He should go. I'm not a good teacher.

His father says she is a wonderful teacher. Andrew agrees. I love learning from you, Mom. But he doesn't mean it. Is he being horrible? Why does he make his mother cry? He doesn't want to hurt her. He walks over and puts his arm around her, but she flinches.

Andrew's dad says, Honey. It's okay. We still have a few weeks to decide.

His mother stands up, wipes away her tears and walks to the bedroom. The door closes behind her.

That night, she skips dinner and goes on a run.

Devin steps outside and immediately drops into a sprint. Her home life is overwhelming enough with her son going off to public school and her husband's possible affair, but the larger world seeps in, and it is all so much weight on already gasping lungs. Devin jogs past a sunset conversation between two men on a beachside bench who talk about the Anthropocene. Somehow, whether or not humans are destroying the Earth is still up for debate in some crowds. The Earth has already begun to lash back with larger storms, more overwhelming heat and cold. Or maybe this isn't a fight. Maybe the Earth is only in its death throes, nervously flailing, struggling to stay alive. It doesn't mean to hurt us, but it can't help itself. Whatever the Earth's intentions, Devin knows it is undeniable that humans are killing it. The Earth must reject us to stay alive.

She passes the bodega, the dealers blatantly lurking in their Cadillac, passes the apartments with shouts rifling through their bedsheet curtains. She keeps running until all conversation is a meaningless mutter at her back, until humans become bodies, and it is just her in the breeze of words, whispers of ocean, and the world a stillness around her.

Her runs become longer, and as summer nears its end, she logs ten miles, stepping out the door after dinner clean up as darkness drops and the children get ready for bed with their father watching over.

She starts out running along Beachfront Boulevard, takes the sidewalk between the highway and the sand. She likes the reassurance of the waves crashing or lapping the shore on one side and the intermittent whoosh of cars on the other, a consistent background at different volumes depending upon the position of the moon and the inclination of the weather as well as the day of the week. But soon, she grows tired of this route and begins to move inland, through the dim-lit streets, past paper-bagged bottles and lusty red-eyed leers. A man calls her honey, and she can't help but smile as she flicks him off, as her heart rate soars with a feeling of risk and drives her on. This is another world. One she hopes her children will never know, but for some reason she feels drawn to with increased curiosity. It is what surrounds their house now that the storms have chased off the vacationers, and even though her husband loves the proletariat, sees working class and slums as real humanity, real life rather than the phony middle- and upper-middle-class assemblage at the Villas, this is still not where she wants her children to wind up, not where she ever hoped to see herself, either. But then again, she thinks, pretty snobbish of her to judge.

It is still hot at night, but she likes the sweat, the slow lick when it trickles down her leg as she steps into her third mile, the way even her hands drip as she clutches her water bottle in one fist, phone in the other.

Though the area is seedy, she feels safe as long as she stays beneath the streetlamps and keeps up a good pace. Stay in the light, like some Bible verse. She has only lived here five years, moving in after the hurricane when Ely's eccentric and aloof uncle left them the house. But five years is enough to know a place if you are careful and pay attention.

What she knows is that there are two versions of her neighborhood, the one before Hurricane Dominic and the one after. The first time she visited Sunport Beach, a few years prior to their move, the city was fairly clean, vacation rentals and large hotels. It was one of many coastal cities: tourist-heavy, seashells and floral shirts, bars playing Jimmy Buffett and serving Singapore Slings and half-priced margs. Dominic had wiped out the oceanfront, though. Since the storm, the rubble had been cleared away with only a few resorts timorously erected to take their place along the savage shore. The minimum wage jobs left with the tourists and the city turned to drugs, to sipping forties on the stoop, to hustling the day away under the blanket of hot, burning sun. Shots fired on a Sunday afternoon. Whatever was necessary to survive. The Sunset Villas miraculously were saved from destruction, but not from the empty hollowness of their current existence.

As Devin considers this, she begins dreaming up dreadful futures for her son and daughter. But then she is too tired to think and lets the subject drop in time to find herself somewhere new, at the edge of a woods with a path that winds into the trees, a deep dark vortex.

She stops in time to hear a cat mew, as it complains its way out of the weeds. It rubs its black side against her leg and she bends down for a pet, feels its ribs through its coat. The cat asks another question and she scratches it behind the ears, rubs the diamond of white on its forehead. She feels comforted, but as she bends to pick it up, the cat runs to the edge of the woods, looks at her, and then trots into the dark. Devin hesitates, but there is nothing to stop her. So she follows.

II.

Their home was a three-year-late wedding gift, but it sometimes feels like a curse. It is a lonely building, a Midwest-style brick two story that stands belligerent against its backdrop of hotels, Doric columns defiant against the pelicans and surfboards and sandy wood porches of other homes. The house belonged to Ely's uncle, a man who, in his retirement, packed mahogany bookshelves with first editions and bought antique furniture, filling his garage with yet-to-be-rehabbed credenzas and rocking chairs. He was the type of man who, when he brought up his land in conversation, mostly talked about how good of a deal he got. He worked in Spokane, engineering bridges for the military until he could collect his retirement. He found this good deal of a property in Sunport and demolished the mobile home that previously hunched on its five acres. It was only a quarter mile from the water in the late '90s, sparse neighbors, but the hotels and Villas, even the water itself, had been creeping closer ever since.

The hurricanes swept in as the years went on and Ely's uncle built a structure to withstand them. To fund his house, he sold most of his acreage to the corporation that built the Sunset Villas, but he was determined to keep his one acre, his home. The 70-year-old man drank scotch, bolstered the house with metal joists, and secured the roof. He watched the rain hit his hurricane-proof windows sideways. Hotels went up around the property. Global Hyatt made an offer on his land and he turned them down. Then another hurricane hit and the Hyatt sold its half-erected luxury suites. In the early 2020s, the consortium of beachfront properties trucked in 15,000 cubic yards of sand to build up the storm-stolen beach. The beachfront residents to the east and west complained that there was gravel in the sand. There was a lawsuit and Ely's uncle sat and read and never visited his family, reclining in his yard in his trunks with a towel tucked behind his head, watching the waves crash and crash and pull the gravelly sand back out to sea.

A strip mall went up in front of the house, and that is when the uncle moved from the porch into politics. He spoke twice before the city council and filed lawsuits. But the strip mall stayed, a drive-through daiquiri joint, a smoke shop, a liquor store, Great Clips. The uncle tucked himself inside then. In the winter, when the sun moved to the south, the building cast a shadow along the front yard. There were dumpsters in front of his house and he would chuck empty bottles at the dumpsters and shout at the hairdressers who took smoke breaks out back.

Finally, Hurricane Dominic swept in and took all of it away, the gravelly sand and the strip mall and the hotels. A Category Five storm with 200-mile-per-hour winds, most of the Gulf was evacuated as Dominic wheeled earthward pushing water into the land, wiping human history from the coast as easily as erasing a footprint. The story was that the entire city was completely evacuated but for Ely's uncle, who sat in his second-story office with a Cuban cigar and his glass of Lagavulin, reading *Moby-Dick* cover to cover by the beam of a battery-operated headlamp. He was a man against nature, an Ahab who would have his whale. It may have been the strip mall that saved him, taking the brunt of the waves, the swell that rose to the second-floor windows. When the water began to recede, the strip mall was rubble, a litter-filled vacant lot. The uncle was asleep and his house still stood.

Now the house looks over the empty lot which the uncle bought himself as a consolation prize for weathering the hurricane. Now the city has struggled back to life. When the wealth went away, it welcomed back its poor. They patched up the brickwork, hammered in new shingles. After the storm, Ely's uncle had a heart attack while wheelbarrowing out loose bricks from the lot. From his hospital bed, the uncle gave up on the house, gifted it to Ely and his bride, Devin. And Ely moved his family into the strongest beachside craftsman ever built, facing the sea like a challenge.

Devin is surprised by how bright the woods actually are when her eyes adjust. The path lies wide as a sidewalk and cleared of weeds. The trees loom, walls of darkness guiding her along a moonlit strip, and the cat curls back to check on her as they move deeper.

The cat mews and Devin watches it swish its arrogant tail. She lets down her hair, then reties it, looks back and can no longer see the empty cul-de-sac, just the blinking yellow of a streetlight as branches wave in front of it. Following the cat, Devin feels at once like she's a hero on a quest as well as a fool chasing a hallucination. More like Don Quixote. Or maybe she is a child in a fairytale, about to be eaten. Whatever the case, she feels like she has no will left in her to fight against this urge onward.

She wonders if the cat wants to lead her to its kittens. She has heard these stories before, where a cat whose children are in a sorry state will seek out human intervention. She wonders why of all people it has chosen her? She is obviously a lousy mother. But, Devin wonders, maybe a kitten is what her family needs. She could surprise Andrew and he would fall in love with it, never wanting to leave the house for school. Plus, a kitten would teach him to take care of something besides himself. Silly thoughts, she knows, these simple hopes that spring out of her and drift off. It is stupid. Her husband is allergic.

Soon, she sees and smells the fire and watches the cat slide into the clearing. Devin stops short in the shadow where she thinks she can't be seen, but then a voice breaks the night.

Hellooo, earthling!

The clearing is a crater in the earth encircled by a knee-high mound of dirt. It is filled with shadows from which the clearing's keeper waves. Devin is spotted, and it is too late to turn and run. She steps forward.

The figure says, Welcome to Tycho, I'm Trinity.

Trinity towers, a giantess in a trench coat and heavy biker boots. She limps and, with the darkness all around, it looks like she lopsidedly floats across the space between them.

Devin says, Tycho?

Named after the crater in the moon, dummy. This is my crater. Creepy, huh?

Trinity smiles, reaches out her open palm, the butt of a hand-rolled cigarette the size of a gun barrel aglow in her mouth. They shake hands.

Devin says, I was following your cat.

Not mine, says Trinity. Nobody owns anybody here. Stella just stops by to visit her kittens. She's a friendly gal, ain't she?

Devin scans the crater. Tycho, like the crater in the moon. It does seem extraterrestrial. The tent is the centerpiece with its flap open to the fire. Two stained, rust-colored lawn chairs along with stumps for sitting. A cooler between the chairs. The ground has been cleared of brush. Evidence of other previous fires in older, darker fire pits pock the periphery. The current fire is ringed with football-sized rocks. The floor of the crater is shadow. Everything above it floats in an eerie light. Devin asks, Is this really an asteroid crater?

Dunno. I have a theory that Stella crashed her ship down here and has been waiting on someone from her home planet to rescue her. Could be anything, really, but I don't want a bunch of *X Files* little shits running all over this place, so I'm trying to keep it on the DL. Right now, it's my home.

Devin says, It's weird. Sorry. She feels the tips of her ears on fire.

Trinity asks, Would you like a PBR? On the house.

Oh, no thanks. Devin says she must be getting back to her run.

Trinity says, Just one fucking beer, babe. Come on. Fuck your husband.

Devin says, How do you know I have a husband?

Trinity measures Devin from her two-week-old Asics, past her naked stomach. She hovers at the sweat on Devin's chest before moving up to the strand of hair that has come loose and dangles beside Devin's left eye. Trinity's gaze lingers again on Devin's scar and Devin feels violated under this stare, shudders through a chill. Trinity winks and turns back to the fire.

Devin follows her and Trinity retrieves a beer from the cooler, cracks it, and hands it over. Trinity says, So, what do you say?

Devin says, I've been running. Sorry. I'm a bit out of it.

Running from what?

Just out for a run. I've been trying to exercise more, get in a good headspace. You know, clear this stuff up. I've just been dealing with a lot.

Trinity blows a raspberry with her mouth, says, Never catch me running for no reason. If I'm running, you better start running with me, 'cause something dangerous is fucking chasing me.

Trinity picks up a leatherbound Bible from the chair next to her, clutches it with one hand around the spine as if about to proselytize. She opens the Bible, sets it on her lap and rips a page out. She says, Cigarette? and waggles the page in Devin's face. Devin shakes her head. Trinity says, You religious?

I was raised that way, but no, not really since college.

Same here.

Trinity pulls a baggie filled with cigarette butts from her jacket pocket. She creases the torn Bible page, sets it in her lap, and rolls each butt between thumb and forefinger, emptying the half-burned tobacco into the paper. She looks at the scripture now covered in fine shake, then she reads: Job 11:1. *Zophar the Naamathite replied...* She says, What a load of bullshit, right? I mean, how can you base your religion on a book with a character named Zophar and not believe that shit's about aliens?

Devin can't keep the laugh from bursting out of her.

Trinity rolls the page into a long cigarette, licks the end, puts it to her lips, lights it. She says, So what's your story, doll?

Devin shakes as if to slough off a heavy burden, the weight of the last few months. She wants to join Trinity in this new, lesser gravity of Tycho. She feels like talking, as if everything, every nightmare within her, is ready for exorcism. Every thought she had during her run rushes back, and maybe it is the beer—she has somehow downed half the can—or maybe it is the moon, or maybe it is the nonchalance of Trinity with her holy cigarette and pure welcome. Maybe it is a dream, but Devin feels the words build up in her mouth like a burp, and she opens up and lets the story belch into the cool air that surrounds this strange other woman.

Devin begins with her son, who no longer wants to be homeschooled. The most recent blow, but then she works her way back. Her marriage to Ely, the most understanding husband. The husband who takes every horror with a kiss, who holds her and tells her they will work through it. She goes back to this aura of Ely, from when they married, and she taught high school while he finished his degree. She tells of moving here with Ely after Hurricane Dominic because his uncle had gifted them the house, and they were too poor to afford even their apartment and Ely took his job here after finishing his Literature MA. She talks about how maybe she never wanted any of this, but it was easier to follow Ely on this absurd dream of being beach bums in this ridiculous world where the beach is eaten away year by year, where the ocean wants to swallow them and everything they have ever built. Devin has become helpless, a sheep tangled in thorns, and she has made Ely some benevolent Jesus-shepherd. His strength makes her feel that much weaker, like she is worthless. Devin pours all of this out of her, treating Trinity like the psychiatrist she never had.

Devin says, I'm treating you like my psychiatrist, I'm sorry.

But Trinity only says, Shit. It's nothing. I've been there too. Left my last husband years ago. Been living off the grid ever since. I'll tell you what I needed to hear then: You've done nothing wrong.

I just can't do it anymore. Everything. I'm ruining myself. I'm ruining my kids. I don't even know if my marriage is real, like, symbiosis, or if it is just codependence, like I'm sick and he's just addicted to helping people. And I can't just leave, but I feel like I really would be much better off on my own without them, and they probably deserve someone who wants to be around them more anyways.

Trinity says, Sometimes the world *can* be all about *you*, you know. You're allowed to be fucking selfish.

Devin doesn't know when she started crying, but Trinity now holds her as more weight weeps out, as her head cleans up its mess of thoughts that have bounced around, accumulated til they choked out the light, these thoughts now flung out into the world.

Trinity says, Shit, girl. You're really in it.

Trinity cracks a second beer and offers it, but Devin is too buzzed already. She takes a sip to be a good guest, but she has already run five miles and is probably dehydrated. Her thoughts fog and cut off, and she struggles to find her words. It is still at least two miles back home. The smoke from Trinity's cigarette washes over her with a craving Devin hasn't felt for years. Trinity asks if she wants to see the kittens.

They walk into the tent, where an air mattress takes up most of the floor and is covered in a wool blanket with a large pillow in the middle, and nestled in the pillow are five kittens, curled and purring. Trinity offers one to Devin and Devin holds her ball of kitten in her hand and feels the bursting beauty of the thing, its softness, its tendency to be broken, and the tears don't flow but dribble out now. They are different tears from before. Not the ones that choke her and never end, but the kind that let all the sorrow out, externalize and rid her of the original sadness. The tears are as welcome as Trinity's embrace.

Devin walks home. She can't run while carrying the kitten, all balled up in a dirty towel and mewling. Anyways, there is too much to process.

She enters through the open garage, walks through the mudroom to the downstairs bathroom and shuts the kitten inside. There is milk in the fridge only rarely, and she empties the last drops of Ely's creamer into a plain white bowl, sets this on the floor in the bathroom as well. She smells the sweat and cigarette smoke on herself. She takes out her contacts, showers as the kitten cries. She brushes her teeth so as not to smell like beer and campfire, and she puts her clothes directly into the washer with extra detergent. It is after midnight and Ely is in bed.

She lies on her side and Ely rolls into her. He mumbles something and she holds him. He asks if she had a good run and she wants to tell him everything, but where even to begin? Her mind feels exhausted, like everything has been drained out. Plus, how can she tell the story without sounding totally selfish and insane?

I was abducted by aliens, she finally says.

Ely chuckles sleepily into her shoulder blade.

Ely never got mad about the kitten, but he was still a bit confused as to why Devin decided to reach down into the drain and pull it out. When she told him this, he wanted to ask for details, but trust is important, so he held his questions. As the children and their mother pooled around the fuzzball, playing with the delicate paws, Ely went out and bought wet food, treats, litter, and a litter box. His eyes itched as he worked on the garage, putting up anything that might harm a small animal, laying down blankets and rugs. This is the plan: the cat can stay in the garage and can come inside only while Ely is at work. Andrew gets online that night and begins dragging cat towers and catnip mice to his wish list. Ely has to admit, as much as it makes his eyes itch, the animal is hard to resist and comfortingly soft.

Ely isn't sure what they will do with the kitten when they go to Cincinnati. He has been planning a family trip to visit his folks. It is August already. In four weeks, Andrew and Layla will start *real* school at Sunport Elementary. In two weeks, Ely's summer session will end and he will have seven days before fall semester picks back up. The trip shouldn't come as a surprise to Devin. Ely brought it up a dozen times since January. He talks about visiting the Newport Aquarium, catching a Reds game with his dad. He mentions Cincinnati to Devin over dinner, though she eats less and less with the family recently, at best only sits at the table with some salad or whittles away at a crust of pizza. He once caught her crumbling bits of cheese in her palm and, later, giving them to the kitten. It is a joke between them that she is worse than the kids. She smiles more with the cat around, which is a good thing. She doesn't seem interested in anything but the kitten and her runs these days, definitely not in Cincinnati.

Ely gets Devin's hesitance to visit his family. The last time she interacted with his folks, Ely's father gripped Devin's hand at the dinner table and asked her to say grace. And this was before her sadness, her days filled with naps. Devin struggled through the prayer, mimicking formal Christian rites, all the familiar phrases, words like *bounty* and *bless*. Then they served ham, potatoes with bacon, green beans with bacon, a pig-heavy feast which Devin, a vegetarian, barely touched. After the meal, Ely's niece, Aleigha, asked Devin why she hadn't closed her eyes during grace, and Devin tried to respond honestly, tried to treat this girl like an adult and give her logical adult answers, then gave up when Aleigha began to cry. Ely listened to his wife say, How would you know my eyes were open if your eyes were closed?

Ely plans the trip on his laptop, propped up in bed with Devin beside him scribbling numbers into a Sudoku book. He shows her a series of hotels, reads reviews aloud. He says,

Check out this one for Red Roof Inn: More like Red Woof
Inn! Because this place has gone to the dogs....He leans into
Devin, turns his computer screen toward her, says, How
about this one, babe?

Devin puts down her Sudoku, says, It's kind of hard to
concentrate with you doing that.

I just thought you might want to help with the hotel. It
has a pool. Sorry.

Devin sighs. No, I'm sorry. I'm just on edge.

Ely wonders: since when have they been apologizing to
each other?

Devin says, What if you just take the kids? You can tell
your family I'm sick. Plus, who's going to snuggle Ornery
every day?

Ely says they can find someone to take care of the cat.
No problem. And why did we even get the cat in the first
place? It's a stray. Take it to the shelter.

Devin scoffs, turns away. We're attached.

Babe, I mean, I know my folks aren't the easiest to get
along with.

I just don't know what I'll do if your dad starts talking
about the *role of women in the church* again. Will he ever get
the fucking point?

Maybe we can talk about it later.

Devin says, And it's not like I ever make you visit my
family.

Okay, says Ely, That's too far. You promised you wouldn't play the dead parent card.

Well, I lied.

Devin rolls over, clicks off the lamp. She is a lump of shadow in the bed beside him, painted by the glow of his laptop screen, the tabs upon tabs of travel websites and cheap hotels. He has been looking forward to this trip for months. They both have, but it feels like Devin veered off at some point, like she is headed somewhere else.

Devin grunts as Ely sits up, bouncing the bed. He doesn't acknowledge the grunt, does not even try to be quiet or ease himself off the mattress. He huffs out of the bedroom, shuffles downstairs into the kitchen, plugs his computer into the charger that Devin's always leaving on the kitchen table, even during meals. He leans back, stares at the screen, and opens his email.

There is no response from the psychiatrist, but it hasn't been twenty-four hours yet. How do you make a loved one seek help? He's typed this question into Google, various keywords, a hundred different variations: "denial of mental illness," which leads him to the word "anosognosia," which is more of a lack of awareness of a mental illness than a denial. There is a wall there, between his wife and her body. He begins to think of her brain as a saboteur bent on tearing her apart, ripping their family to shreds. He searches "mental illness intervention," finds a ten-step guide to successful procedures. There is a company listed with an 1-800 number: Professional interventionist. He bookmarks the page, but it seems so strange that there are those who make their living off of talking people into going places they don't want to go or getting help they don't believe they need. Fucking capitalists! He takes off the bookmark. How could he be so lazy? This is his job as her husband, her best friend. They trust each other. It should be him.

The thought crosses his mind, *is this really my wife?* She could have been abducted either by aliens or by humans, lab experiments to alter her brain chemistry. He has been watching too much Mulder and Scully. Men in white coats, naked aliens with ginormous cat's eyes. The question must be asked, *Am I, Ely, the one who is suffering from mental illness?*

His email dings faintly in the background, a distraction he latches onto, this contact with the outside world bringing him back to the present.

The message is from a student. Not just any student, but Cassie, the shining star of last semester's otherwise indifferent eight-student Early Novel course. Cassie schedules meetings with him for every paper, listens diligently to his suggestions, talks with him while he packs up after class. She bounces around theories and interpretations of the present text. It was Cassie who wrote an essay on the influence of book-making methods during the time that Henry Fielding wrote *Joseph Andrews*. But Cassie is on break. There is no meeting coming up, no reason for her to shoot off an email after midnight during the summer before going into her senior year. It is exciting and nerve-racking.

He looks around the room and clicks on the email:

*Ely, I just signed up for your American Literature course for
the fall and I was wondering if you have the book list yet?*

Thanks,

Cassie

407-926-1060

Is Ely the one with the unstable mind? Why does his
student feel comfortable using his first name? Why give him
her number? He imagines meeting with Cassie. She is
twenty-one years old, he recalls. Why does he care about her
age? He is her teacher. He has no other intentions but to
teach. *Cassie, I can't. I have a sick wife. I have kids.* But what
is it that he *can't?* A married man with children, a sick wife.
How can he say that his wife is even sick? Is his wife even his
wife anymore? And what of Cincinnati? His wife, at the
moment, feels like an albatross around his neck. A beautiful
albatross that he cares for so much that it hurts. An albatross
that doesn't ever want sex anymore.

He never imagined he could want anything more than
he had until this moment. He thought he could take care of
his family, just be kind and buoy the family with his
goodwill, but she won't give an inch for him. She is selfish.
Now he wants anything else.

The next morning, Ely reaches over the gate and lifts the
handle, squeaks the wrought iron open and the kids follow
him to the pool. They have been swimming in the early
mornings because the algae blooms are back and the entirety
of Beachfront Boulevard reeks of dead fish. It is not safe to
swim in the ocean. But as they approach the poolside, Layla

stops and says, Dad. There's no water. And she is right. The pool has been drained and dead lizards float in the scum with palm fronds, sand, and dirt. The pool cleaning robot is upside-down on the tiles.

How many days has it been? It seems like they were just there, bobbing around playing Marco Polo, and now there is nothing. Ely says, Hold on. Hold on. I'm calling Carl.

Carl, the maintenance man for the Sunset Villas, says he is sorry, but there just aren't enough guests to keep it open.

What about me? says Ely. I'm a guest.

Carl snorts through the phone, wind whooshing into the speaker. He must be driving. Carl says, What villa are you staying in?

I'm in—Ely scouts the address on the nearest house—202 Palm Heart Drive.

Ely. I know it's you. There's only two families in the whole place right now. That's it.

Ely says, Do you know when they'll fill it again?

Carl says, No clue. I'm sorry, man. But there's nothing I can do.

The kids rush back to the house with this news for Devin. She listens to their simultaneous stories while she strokes the kitten who naps on its back. She doesn't emote, barely listens as Layla says, Whatever will we do?!

So Ely tells them not to worry. Red Tide won't last forever. They will figure something out.

At the mouth of the path to Tycho, Devin hesitates. She wears her new tank-top with high-waisted leggings, a headlamp that she beams down the break in the brush. She walked the last mile so she won't show up too sweaty. She feels ridiculous. Who is she trying to impress?

A few steps across the treeline and she stops, turns back. It is 10:00 p.m., the sun is gone, its red-at-night glow settled into the Gulf, calming the waves. Devin knows that she is not a brave person. It has taken her a week to work up the courage to even come this far. Devin is still baffled that she didn't sprint out of the woods as soon as she saw that someone lived in this crater called Tycho. She must have been dehydrated, not thinking right. It isn't like Devin to be brave or stupid or whatever she was that night she brought home her little kitten cure. She is astonished that she drank a beer offered by a stranger. She thinks *This is how a woman gets raped or murdered. This is why they never find the body.* But, once again, she enters the woods, clicks off the headlamp, follows the shadow outline of the path by the light of the moon. She keeps looking over her shoulder to make sure no one is following.

How many other women have wandered off into the woods and been lost to the world?

How many abductions have occurred here?

How many husbands have woken up with their wives gone, never to see or hear from them again?

How many would just move on? How many deserve to miss their wife forever?

Trinity is firelit, cocked back in her chair like a lazy trigger never squeezed, but she rises to greet Devin: My good bitch! I hoped I would see your fine ass again.

Devin tells Trinity all about her argument with Ely while Trinity underhands a PBR in her general direction and the fire rushes and swirls in its pit. It doesn't make sense for Devin to go to Cincinnati. She has Ornery to care for, her own life to worry about. She drinks another PBR while she cries about the email she saw on Ely's laptop this morning. Devin says, I mean, what fucking nerve to even be flirting like that with my husband. I don't know. I thought he was different but men just go around taking what they want. They want to make us comply. She says, I hate his family, every one of them.

Trinity says, Some would say that if he's thought about fucking her, then it's just as bad as doing it, whether or not he's, you know, hit that shit.

This doesn't help anything. But Devin doesn't flinch, either. She doesn't ask the real question, the one that has crescendoed to the point that it has blotted out all emotional response: Does she really even care? More than an affair, Devin is afraid of having to act for Ely's family, to be the perfect mother, to interact with her children who she feels are becoming more distant by the day, more difficult to figure out. Does it matter if Ely has another life, relationships she doesn't know about?

Trinity says, You know why you're happy here? Now?

Devin says, What do you mean?

I mean, Trinity lights a cigarette torn from the Book of Revelation, You like it here because you get to be you for you, not anybody else. She takes a puff. And because you're attracted to me.

Trinity laughs out smoke.

They walk through the woods on Devin's third PBR, a path that leads away from the road, curls back to a beach Devin never even knew existed. The moon's pull on the ocean is a pull on the spirit as well, its light ominous and auspicious. Devin feels the lift.

Then Trinity takes off her clothes. She stands in her underwear, ball of jeans and trench coat under her arm. She says, Care for a swim?

There is no algae bloom here, as if it is a different world altogether, a different space and time. In Devin's younger years, when she was an artist, or at least went to school for art, she would jam Pere Ubu and lose herself in acrylic color. In a way, she could enter her painting, drift away to alternate realities. She gets the same feeling from this beach, another dimension, another date and landscape. She asks, Where even are we?

It's Tycho Beach. It's secret. No one can find it except me.

There is no dead fish smell. The breeze comes in off the water salty and fresh. She notices that there are no waves, no surf. The glass is still, barely rippled.

The beer Devin drank has given her a permanent smile that twitches at the corner as she stares at Trinity, the loose gut swaying unashamed in the moonlight, arms that sag. She looks older than Devin, but has the energy of someone much younger. There is a freshness in the way that she speaks and there is a vertical scar, faded but still present, a pale ghost of when life was pulled out of her. Trinity proudly embodies so much of what Devin is afraid of. Trinity tucks her clothes under the bench and runs along the sand to the water, keeps running until she is tripped by the knee-deep pull of it, smacks into the pool and disappears.

Devin strips quickly, expertly executes a shallow dive. When she comes up for air, she gags. Trinity dunks Devin under and they both break the surface sputtering. Devin swims away down the beach, leaving Trinity alone. There is a danger here that keeps the blood flowing, the limbs moving. There is something bigger than Devin playing with her, pulling her out further then pushing her back. She can go wherever the water takes her, needs nothing but to float.

When Devin returns to her friend, Trinity is staring blankly back at her clothes on the beach. Devin grabs her arm and Trinity shakes her head. They swim out a bit further and tread water, but Trinity keeps guarding her belongings, distracted.

When they finish swimming, they drip-dry on the bench. It is going on midnight and both women yawn into the constellations, the blinking lights of barges way out. It's all light and darkness, constant noise of waves breathing in the background. Trinity says, You can ask about my scar. I've seen you looking. But then, you have to tell me about yours.

Devin touches her cheek where a man once hurt her, 15 years ago, a different life. A scar so much a part of her that she mostly forgets that it is there.

Mine, Devin says, was just a man. That's all. A man long gone and never again.

Trinity touches her own scar, Mine's the same story. A man long gone, never coming back.

Ely has spent two weeks building up the courage to talk to his wife, and today he is ready. He doesn't play music in the car on the way home, just thinks and drives. He is so thoroughly stuck in his head playing out both sides, self-editing his approach, that he doesn't know if he ran that red light or not. His window is cracked so he doesn't overheat. The air is muggy, a throatful of heat and funk thick enough to gargle. It still reeks of dead fish, though the bloom has gone its own way. He adjusts the seatbelt over his growing gut. He hasn't been to the gym in weeks. Between coming back early to take care of the kids and worrying about Devin, he has let himself go, forgotten.

Every day, he walks through the door to see his wife sitting on the couch petting the kitten as if the world has disappeared and she is the only thing in it. Or she naps in the bedroom, neither serene, nor especially sorrowful, only weary. She needs a hand to help her up.

He has a doctor lined up to see Devin. He has already met with the doctor once, and though the doctor won't discuss diagnoses prematurely, he believes Devin does need help. Still, Ely is nervous. He feels like anytime he has brought something up around Devin, she has either been angry or just completely broken down.

A few days ago, he mentioned the running at night. She keeps getting home later and later. Ely always pretends to sleep, but he feels the way the bed shifts when she slides in next to him at midnight smelling like her citrus body wash and toothpaste. He knows she isn't fucking anyone, but why would she do her laundry every night? And why is she getting home so late? If she was running the whole time, she would be clocking in slow marathons. Her only answer has been that she sometimes likes to sit for a while and cool off. He doesn't think she's cheating. He also knows she's too anxious to go out and meet people. When he asks her another morning, after the night he caught a faint whiff of cigarettes on her, she tells him she is stressed, and why can't he just trust her? He wants to trust her. He pretends the cigarette smell away. She says, Are you sleeping with someone? Is this just projection?

So, Ely has backed off. He tucks the children into bed at night while Devin dresses in her running gear, does her stretches. He reads to the children from *Charlotte's Web* while Devin jogs off into the night. He plans the trip to Cincinnati by himself. Grades papers. Talks to doctors. Does his Google searches. Wonders if Devin will even come home at all. How much more of this can any of them take? No matter how unhealthy it is to sit back and let his frustration build, he wants to allow her the space to be who she is, but recently this space crushes him.

The real problem came a few days ago when Ely's son asked him why Mom isn't around anymore. She's around, Ely says, during the day.

Andrew says, But she's always sleeping or reading a book, or she locks herself in her room and just tells us to play.

All of that is why Ely can't pretend any longer. By the time he gets home, he has the discussion all mapped out. First, he cooks dinner. While Devin gets ready for her run, he puts the kids to bed and tells them to read to themselves, just for tonight. He waits on the couch, watching Devin stretch and ignore him. Finally, Devin stands, raises her hands high. Ely says, Babe, I think it's time to see a psychiatrist. He blurts it out. It's almost too easy.

She says, No. No. I'm fine.

He says, Babe. It's not fine.

And Devin breaks down. She collapses into his chest in tears. She says, I am such a horrible mother and wife! Why can't I do anything right?

He wants to tell her to stop. Then he wants to shake her and walk out and never come back. He wants to tell her how selfish she is, how she doesn't get to ignore everyone else and do whatever the fuck she feels in the name of self-care. He wants to shove her off of his lap. But he just trembles, says instead, It's just whatever is going on with you now. It's something we need to maybe get some help with.

Devin collapses like a demolished building. Her armature can't hold her.

She responds only in sobs. She doesn't want help. She has her nightly runs. He needs to understand.

Ely tries to wrap himself around her, to tell her it is nothing she did, but her hurt is so strong that she breaks from him, can't even look her husband in the eye when she says she needs to go. He tries not to sound hurt, but the pain is there in the reverberations of his Okay.

He says, Go on, babe. Just fucking go.

Ely, she says, I'm sorry. Just give me time. Try to understand.

Devin stops at the bodega on her way to Tycho and runs three miles with a muffuletta hoagie gripped in her left fist and a 24 oz. PBR in her right. She doesn't know if Trinity is vegetarian or not, but either way, a muffuletta is a safe bet.

When she reaches the clearing, Devin holds the sandwich and beer high and shouts out, Greetings from Earth!

Then she watches the figure of Trinity pop up from her chair and look around wildly saying, Who are you? What the fuck do you want? If you're a cop, you have to tell me. But then a smile shears across her face and she opens herself up for a hug.

Devin says, I was just running by and I thought you might be hungry.

My bitch. Hey. You came just in time to see my new baby.

Devin hands Trinity the hoagie and the beer, and Trinity cracks the can, spraying foam onto her shirt. She sucks the beer out, looks up and winks at Devin. She puts the drink in the cupholder. Trinity says, Sit down, I'll be right out.

When she emerges from the tent, there is a baby raccoon on Trinity's shoulder. She says, What do you think? Named him Alf. He's really quite an Alf, isn't he?

Devin is shocked into giggles. Isn't he the cutest thing? Are you going to tame him?

Trinity says, There's no taming a raccoon. He'll become wild soon enough. They always do. The thing about raccoons is, you think they're gonna be nice and cute and hang around forever, and then they hit adulthood and bite the shit out of you and run off. Kinda like me, you know. I become an adult and go wild. Just like you, kinda.

Devin thinks about this. She hates when people compare human interactions to those of animals. Nature doesn't have some unadulterated control over her. Devin says, I guess, but I don't know.

Trinity lights a Biblical cigarette. She says, Let me tell you. I tried to stay with my husband for nine years and it never got any better. I felt caged in. I'd tell him he didn't deserve me. Told him every time we were out that all these dudes were measuring me up, checking me out. When he tried that shit on me and said someone was checking him out, then, I told him he was delusional. Told him he was fat and stupid. It's dumb, but I wanted him to hurt. I wanted him to hurt so bad so that he wouldn't need me. Nine years and I was just done with married life, living in the same house trying to care for him and myself. And I hurt him because I didn't realize I could get out. Then I just left. Kindest thing I've ever done. I saw him once. He was out with another lady and he looked happy. Sometimes it's just best to separate. For everyone.

Devin drinks. She says, Not Ely. He would die if I left, drink poison or throw himself on his sword. Something Shakespearean.

Fuck Shakespeare, says Trinity. Everyone thinks he's the shit but he's just another cocky white dude.

The raccoon nibbles on Trinity's ear. Devin stares, pondering. She says, I just think it might be different for me. I mean, I love my family. I even like them. It's my duty to take care of them even when it wears me out.

Trinity says, Well, as your psychiatrist, I'm prescribing at least twice weekly visits to Tycho then, and at least two beers a night. If the hubby gives you any shit, tell him you wear the pants.

Devin takes a long swig.

Trinity says, I can never remember, is it -chiatrist or -ologist that prescribes meds?

I can't remember either for some reason. Whatever it is, though, it's working.

Devin follows Trinity's advice. She visits more frequently, every couple nights, sometimes bringing beer, once a bag of bagels snagged from the dumpster behind the convenience store.

Trinity takes a bite of bagel, shows Devin the inscription in the front of the Bible: *May you learn to see the way of the Lord. Love, Mom and Dad.*

This makes Devin want to cry. Trinity's family is gone but their words are still with her, still pushing her away.

A couple hours later, she is in the shower. She washes off the loneliness, smiles because she has a friend in Trinity. She falls asleep on the couch.

She sleeps on the couch again the next night, begins to make a habit of it. She has slept on the couch for over a week now because it is somewhat comfortable and she doesn't wake up Ely and he hasn't said anything about it. He doesn't have much to say at all these days. When he is in the kitchen, she reads on the porch or sits in the garage with the cat who is now eleven pounds and likes to dig his claws into Devin's leg. When Ely takes the kids to the beach, she does the crossword in bed. When he is away at work and Devin is home with the children, she takes long naps. Her nights get later, but also, her body seems to need more rest than usual.

—

During another walk from Tycho to Trinity's mystical beach, Trinity stops in her tracks, pounces, and comes up with a black snake held just below the jaw. On Trinity's face, the waxing crescent of a grin.

The tent is filled with kittens that grow and roam around the fire. Devin and Trinity feed them bits of jerky from the bag Devin brings.

Devin's cat grows plump. The children like to carry the cat under their arms around the yard and Ornery doesn't even complain as long as he is fed.

Devin brings a bag of cat food to Tycho and the bag is raided by raccoons later in the night, Meow Mix scattered through the woods.

When Devin was in college, she felt alone, lost, kept loving the wrong people again and again. She thought her relationship with Ely would change everything, would fill her life, but had it?

The trip to Cincinnati is imminent and they still haven't spoken about it. Ely still calls Devin honey, still kisses her head before he leaves, but he doesn't press her on anything, doesn't even bring it up, and she is the one who feels guilty.

Trinity draws a map of the United States in the sand. They are stoned, Devin from only one hit of the joint, Trinity still puffing away. Trinity marks an X in every state where she has lived. The two women are about the same age but seem to survive along different timelines. Trinity might be in her forties but with a face unlined, unplaceable. She relives her life, her affairs, leaving one town, disappearing, people in her wake grieving and forgetting. Trinity says she is not sure where she will go next.

Devin mouths, Next?

Well I can't stay here forever.

HURRICANE TRINITY

Trinity pulls a bottle of Jack Daniels from the iceless cooler. Says, It's my birthday. Drink.

—

The day before they are supposed to leave for Cincinnati, Devin is a bit hungover from the whiskey, and her mind is clouded from the weed. Ely left her asleep on the couch without a word, only a note on the table. It is almost noon and the house is empty. Devin is still in her running clothes, can smell the booze on her own breath. The note says, *Canceled class and took the kids to the zoo today. Thought you may need the time to yourself. Can we talk tonight? I'm worried, babe. Text so I know you're okay. —Ely*

Devin feels like pure failure and doesn't eat breakfast. She gets in her car since her head hurts too much to run, and she drives to the convenience store where she buys a red pack of Pall Malls—an uneducated guess—and two Gatorades. She downs one of the Gatorades on her way to the woods. As she drives, she ponders over the phrasing of Ely's note. No *love*, not even a *Honey*, just a *babe* like they are in high school. She has never been more afraid of a conversation. Is there anything she hasn't ruined? How the fuck can she even begin to explain? Hangovers are the physical manifestation of regret exploding. In Tycho, Devin thinks, she can find answers.

She reaches the path and parks a little way down the street where the sandy berm is wider. She drinks half of the second Gatorade in one gulp, feels a little bit better. The sun makes the shut off car a sauna. The sun has been getting hotter, hanging lower over the Gulf than ever before. She walks toward the path. She has never seen it in the daytime before, but it all looks so bare, so blatant and honest.

When she reaches the blank face of Tycho, Devin deposits the pack of cigarettes and finishes the drink. There is no note here, which is what she expected. Trinity couldn't say it and neither could Devin, even though they both talked all those hours into the night. Trinity is extremely gone, a memory that will most likely fade, a scar that will one day go away. Or not. Whatever the case, Devin is utterly alone.

On the drive home, she cries herself through fond memories, pictures of the two of them passing the time. Her life has ended and she doesn't know what's next.

To say she is depressed is to chew a mere bite out of the soggy sandwich that is Devin's existence. It is more than merely missing Trinity. Maybe it's envy. Maybe Devin wishes that, like Trinity, she could leave everything behind, be a person alone in the world, completely satisfied with herself. Maybe it is something so much more complex that she can't even begin to fathom, and maybe this inability to fathom what she feels is itself the void she falls into. The crashing wave background noise becomes the rush of a hurricane, everything flying too fast to cling to.

And it only gets worse. Every little lie, each slip-up, the time she turned her back to check out the Sunset Villa flowers when she should have been watching her children at the beach. These are strikes against her, or like little weights she's been adding to the bag strung around her neck. If she could take those weights with her, walk from the car across the highway, step out onto the beach and keep stepping into the ocean—but she can hardly make it from her car through the front door.

She doesn't know time. She collapses, muddy shoes, burden of guilt and all, and waits for judgment to come down. She is ready to burn. And then she hears the door creak open and Andrew, her beautiful, troubled son runs over to her, slams a pizza box on the coffee table three feet from her face, and he says with a flourish of his hands, Mother! Dinner is served! She bursts into tears all over again, fat amphibians of grief moving up her throat, into her mouth.

Andrew tries to hug her, frightened but with open arms, and it is all she can do to shake her head rather than hit him, reach her arm out to fend off his easy forgiveness. They should take her out and stone her. It would hurt less than her children's love. Layla stands in the doorway and splats her pizza box on the floor, then collapses beside it. Layla doesn't know why she is crying and neither does Devin, and this similarity makes hope harder for Devin to grasp.

Ely herds the kids off into the kitchen with their dinner and sits on the couch. He puts a hand on her thigh. Looks concerned. Says nothing.

After a few moments, she finds her voice, says, Who the fuck cries over pizza? What the fucking fuck is wrong with me?

And Ely jumps his head at the word "fuck" because she has never really cursed much around him.

She says, Pizza is supposed to be the happiest thing in the world.

That night, she lies in bed, but can't sleep so she goes back to the couch and cries on and off, hates herself, wants to die. But then she has visions. Ely finds her on the couch with wrists gushing, rivers tributarying to the blood-ocean of the carpet. What does he tell the kids? There's no solution that won't destroy her children further. She feels the dream noose around her neck tighten, but she could never follow through on something so emotionally damaging.

She wonders, What if I just left? She would need only a couple thousand dollars in cash to make it to the other side of the country. Find a job, be a waitress, or in sales, something just enough to eke by and be away from anyone she could hurt. She could change her name. So much overwhelming work.

How selfish, she thinks, to even have the idea of killing myself. Also, she realizes she is selfish and she can't not be selfish. She is in no position to do anything for anyone else. She wants to live, but doesn't know how or what she should be.

The next day is Saturday. They should be leaving for Cincinnati and Devin still can't get up. Ely sets breakfast in front of her, feels her forehead, which isn't warm. He asks if he can take her to the hospital.

Devin says nothing.

Ely leaves her, takes the kids, and comes back alone. The day is a blur. It is the end of her life. Ely has the largest suitcase in his hand and stands in front of the couch.

They both cry on the way to the hospital, but Devin doesn't recognize the route.

Tears run out. Devin is deadpan. This is supposed to be something drastic. She wants to throw her phone out the window, a symbol of cutting all ties, a symbol of disappearing. But what would that do to the environment? She wants to scream and kick and make him drag her because it is his fault. But she doesn't have the energy to fight the kindest man she has ever hurt, who has never hurt her and never meant to.

How are you feeling, honey? This is no big deal. It happens. We'll fix it. I love you. Everyone loves you.

This has happened before: Sylvia Plath, Anne Sexton, Zelda Fitzgerald. Others have survived it.

This is the end of the end.

Feels like it is over.

III.

Almost a decade later, in his senior year of high school, Andrew wins best in show at the art fair with a watercolor piece, sunset in the Gulf, a rainbow, the ocean when its waters are at their stillest. It is a calm scene, the seashore before it was washed away by the latest act of God: Hurricane Cherise. But in this painting, there are also blank patches that disrupt the clean lines. In the bottom left corner there is a sloppy, black smudge, then another a few inches up. The art is marred and unfinished. He has named the drawing, *The Saddest Day on Earth*, and no matter how much his teacher wants him to change the title so that it matches the beauty she sees, he won't, and as much as she wants him to clean up the smudges, he insists that she just doesn't get it. He doesn't think it is such a difficult concept to grasp that the world is sometimes flawed and still lovely.

When Devin sees the piece, she tears up and hugs Andrew, says, Oh my God! I have the most talented son in the world. And Andrew scans the room over her shoulder to make sure none of his friends are watching. Then he hugs her back hard.

On the drive home, Andrew sits in the rear seat, Devin up front, window cracked, because the new medication makes her car sick. Layla has only had her permit for 3 weeks and Devin clutches the Oh-Shit-Handle above the door and applies imaginary passenger-side brakes that don't work fast enough. Andrew tells Layla that the stop signs with the white borders are optional, but the black border means mandatory. He ducks his mother's playful smacks. Don't tell her that!

It is one month until Andrew's graduation and then he is off to Columbus, Ohio to study art at his mother's alma mater. What are the odds that he would follow in Devin's footsteps? He is excited to meet new friends, to dig deep into his craft. He has become an avid reader like his mother, even dabbles in poetry. He looks forward to this new life in which he can spend all of his time creating.

He remembers so little of the day his mother went to the hospital. He hadn't known the details then, only that his mom who once hovered over his shoulder had slowly faded into the background. She didn't come back until he was already entrenched in schoolwork and surrounded by friends. He remembers visiting her, being frightened to see so many people underdressed, milling around on the smooth and sanitized fourth floor of the hospital. He remembers that Layla began to cry the moment they stepped through the sliding glass door. Layla was confused. She wondered if their mother was going to die. The sad face his mother gave him, the pursed lips, the waxy sunlessness of her. The nurses in their scrubs bore a seriousness that, mixed with the confused and tired bodies of the patients, gave off the aura of final years.

Then his mother was home and everything was different. She didn't help with school. His dad was around more, leaning over the table to show Andrew how to decipher his math homework or direct him to the space where the adverb goes while diagramming a sentence. There was a time when he was younger that he remembered his mom lining up chocolate chips, one for each problem, a reward for his work, but the memory became so faint, so unlike the present, that he wonders if he imagined it. Now his mom sits on the couch much of the day reading and nodding out with the cat loafed up like a ship at her feet.

Now Layla and Andrew drive themselves to school. They only really see each other in the car ride to and from. Layla always lingers with her friends, forcing Andrew to wait in the parking lot long after the bell while she laughs with a group around her, all white teeth, all legs and short running shorts. Layla is a runner and Andrew is a walker. When they get home on nice days, Andrew plods what is left of the beach now that the shipment of sand has been swept back out and the city has no money to replace it. Layla jogs by on the street. Andrew remembers his mom going on late night runs back before she was sick. Running annoys him. He'd rather step slowly, take in the surf, the beach growing and receding. Breathe in, breathe out, watch the dolphins arc and jostle along the coast.

It is an undeniable truth that the Earth is changing. Six years after Devin started her first antidepressant, the state government began a project to move the highway back another fifty yards from the ocean. Then, before the plan was underway, Hurricane Cherise bombed the shore and the sand was swept out to sea along with many other seaside buildings. Tourism plummeted once again. The Villas went up for sale and never sold. That winter was the coldest on record. The Sunset Villas never rehired Carl and the pool was never filled. Half the houses were still windowless, half-clad in vinyl siding. Of course, their house still stands, a testament to manic engineering. The waves receded after the storm, but Beachfront Boulevard was destroyed and they detoured the road even further inland to meet up with the highway. Traffic stays clear of the house now. In the summer, the sun feels like a death-ray, and the heat is so oppressive that Ely lets the car run with the A/C on until it is cool enough for him to drive to work.

It is so hot that Layla only runs at night, getting home late, sometimes smelling like beer, glowing of her first kiss and subsequent kisses. Sometimes she complains about where they live. She wants to move somewhere less *ghetto*.

If they ever were to sell the house, they have missed their chance. Homes close to the beach are worthless these days, the land sacrificed a yard a year or more to the rising sea.

Within their lifetime, they will be underwater.

Eventually, they have to visit Ely's parents in Cincinnati. Since the day of the incident that sent her to the hospital,

Devin jokes that Cincinnati brought on her depression. I mean, she says, How can you *not* develop severe depression when thinking about Cincinnati? She makes the excuse, With all these pills I gotta take with me, we'd have to book an extra seat on the plane.

Enough time has gone by since her stay at the hospital for the joke to bring a smile to both her and Ely's faces. Ely has been busy these intervening years. On her medication, Devin isn't always the most dependable driver. Her vision sometimes blurs, her hands sometimes shake. For years, one drug cocktail after another, some put her to sleep while on others she spends the night wandering the house in a fugue. With these excuses, he steps down from his position of head of the English Department, cancels trips back home to see his family. He has been taking care of the kids, driving his wife to the doctor. His parents come to Sunport to visit and stay in an inland hotel. They tell jokes about the crazy beach-house-building uncle. Once, as the rumor goes, he bought a monkey that ravaged the house and ran off with his favorite pocket watch. They sit around the dining room table with bizarre tall-tales and exaggerations. They all laugh together. Devin carves a tiny tofurkey and Ely, graciously, says the prayer.

But during her eleventh year on medication, Devin does cede, finally, to take the trip to Cincy for her in-law's 50th anniversary. It is September and the kids are both off to college, Andrew in his junior year of art school and Layla in her first year of culinary school in North Carolina. Devin feels a bit down, the usual empty-nester-type down, nothing like before. She packs Monday through Wednesday pills into marked canisters and stuffs them into her carryon.

It is just her and Ely, and nothing interesting happens in Cincinnati. Her father-in-law takes them out to dinner at a fancy restaurant and Devin doesn't order wine. She snaps a Klonopin in half and swallows it before the main course comes. At another meal, Devin is able to say the prayer without meaning, but with enough verve to please the Presbyterians. They don't even bring up her depression because, she realizes, it is no longer what defines her. They tell her that she looks fit, which she knows is a lie. She's put on 30 pounds that she still can't quite come to terms with and she can't keep off no matter how much exercise. The trade-off of heft for a quality of life is worth it, so she doesn't complain out loud. They stay two nights, and while Ely's dad drives them back to the airport, it begins to snow.

Ely's dad says, Snow in September? I'll be darned.

As soon as the plane lands in Biloxi, Devin opens her phone to a message from Andrew's college. She calls back and, after many holds and transfers, she reaches the health clinic who say that Andrew swallowed an entire bottle of anti-anxiety pills. They found him just in time. There was foam at the mouth, a seizure. Andrew is alive, thank God. Devin wants to know what kind of pills. But they don't have an answer. Devin lets the phone fall to the floor, slumps on the bench. Somewhere around her, above her, Ely asks, What is it? What's wrong?

She says, Did you know Andrew was taking medication?
She is in a daze all the way to the shuttle and she dozes
during the entire trip home. The next day, they decide Ely
should fly to Columbus to escort Andrew back to Sunport.
Devin has an appointment with her psychiatrist in the
morning. She needs to stay. She doesn't think she can travel
anyways. Ely books his ticket, takes off the next morning.

Andrew can't explain it, though nobody asks him to answer
for what happened. He tells the psychiatrist that, yes, he did
mess around with substances a bit: pot a few times at parties,
Captain Morgan one night and blacked out in someone else's
bathtub. But for the last year, he has been totally sober. He
has just felt short of desire. He scheduled his classes for later
in the day with the idea that a bit of sleeping-in would help,
but he still found himself cocooned in sheets at noon, unable
to will his body into motion.

He became anxious around people too. There was an
incident at Walmart when the lights began turning on him
like UFO tractor beams and everybody seemed to stare, so he
sprinted out of the place, through the parking lot, and sat in
his car trying to slow his breathing so he wouldn't die,
breathing in and out through an empty Wendy's bag. His
girlfriend was worried, so he dumped her with the baseless
excuse that he needed the time alone to concentrate on his
school work. He broke into a sweat, overwhelmed by a

syllabus. He only finished half a page on his fifteen-page final paper, and the bouquet of blown glass flowers he was working on cooled too fast and shattered while Andrew imagined terrible ways for himself to die. He wanted his girlfriend's company, but couldn't bring her down with him.

The school psychiatrist prescribed the Xanax based on the Walmart incident, ignoring the other symptoms as mere sadness over a breakup. Downing a bottle of Xanax made sense at the time, not meant to be an extravagant gesture, but a way to end it, to remain unmoving, or at least to force something, anything to change. His body wanted stillness. He wanted to be nothing.

Of course, he researched other methods of suicide. Back in Sunport, once he starts seeing a new psychiatrist, it all spills out. The first time was in second grade when he tied a bungee cord into a knot, hooked it on a support beam and tied it around his neck, but there was too much give. The psychiatrist, of course, keeps this to himself and prescribes recommended doses, promises they will work through this.

Andrew gets into the habits of new medication, looks at the last month of his search history on his MacBook. There are enough sappy breakup songs on his Spotify to choke the happiest man on Earth. Then there are searches for ways to kill himself. There are questions about how much time passes during the attempt, what he would see, hear, feel. He had even joined a chat room where the members discussed failed attempts, sharing wisdom of how to do it right, how you should place a bag over your head after swallowing the Xanax to cut off the air supply and rush into death more quickly. He doesn't remember why he never used a bag.

Andrew erases his history. Back in his childhood house in Sunport, he paints canvases in the evenings and compares antidepressants and their interactions with his mom.

For Devin, the following year is an obstacle course of mood-altering medications. SSRIs, anxiolytics, antipsychotics. Her blood pressure spikes and she's given a drug for that. She's told to stop drinking alcohol, so she stops. They say that happens when you age. Your body changes. Everything is altered. The same meds begin to act differently. Then another doctor tells her a glass of wine at night may help her sleep, so she sips Sauv Blanc with her meals. They give her Ambien, and she wakes up groggy from a twelve-hour hibernation believing that she has strangled her husband. But then Ely is in the kitchen with Starship Enterprise-shaped pancakes and they share an adorable moment together, just the two of them over an intergalactic breakfast. Sometimes, the best care is having nowhere to go that day, sitting with a book, a cat, and people who love her. She dreads sleep but, once again, the pills begin to help with that.

She is glad that Andrew is back home. The school granted him medical leave for as long as he needed it. He can go back at any time, but for now, he and Devin are inseparable. When Ely goes off to work and Devin sinks into the anhedonia of the couch, Andrew drags her by the hand out the door, across the cracked and unused pavement of the old Beachfront Boulevard, and they go on walks along the water, sometimes both of them dripping tears the entire time, bringing up super-nostalgic memories.

When Andrew turns 21 later that year, he says he doesn't want a party, just wants to stay in. Even with all of his progress, he hasn't come to terms with big crowds, and neither of them want to drive the half hour inland to the nearest decent club anyways. So they walk to the liquor store and buy a twenty-dollar red blend. Then they sit on the back deck and Devin watches, holding in a laugh as Andrew takes his first legal sip of booze and sputters it out back into the glass. Never has he tasted something so dry. He says it makes his entire esophagus squint.

She says, It's no Arbor Mist, is it? and Devin goes in and opens a bottle of sugary Moscato, a long-ago gift that has been gathering dust in the cabinet. They celebrate. It is not always tears and anxiety. Often, it is joy.

Time goes by and Devin begins to hate dry red wine too. The doctor puts her on lithium and this seems to be the solution. Of course, most wine tastes like iron, like blood. Also, she now can't stand the flavor of anything pickled. It reminds her of the smell of hot tar, fresh asphalt. Everything evens out, but her hands shake. Her blood pressure still rises, but when it does, she takes a pill.

Layla stays at home over the summer and mothers both Devin and Andrew as they struggle to find stasis. From North

Carolina, Layla brings culinary school recipes, techniques of dicing and frying, a whole energy of cooking. She even sautés fancy dishes for the new cat, Fingerlickin, who replaced Ornery after his cremation. Layla is all cheer, pure joy, and she gives her energy freely.

Andrew finds the right cocktail of meds to go out in public again, gets a job live-painting for tourists in Florida. He runs wine and paint events for small groups at a tap room in Mobile. He begins talking about reenrolling in classes come spring.

And Ely supports them somehow, through his hard work, his care with savings. He finds time to go on runs with Devin. They cut along the beach, then back through town, and Devin begins to lose some of that superfluous, depressive weight that used to bother her. When she pinches her belly to make it talk to her in the mirror, it is not demeaning, its mouth so thin that it seems at a loss for words. Here, with her family, Devin holds onto life like the precious confetti of moments it is, beautiful even as they float off or are sogged by rain.

Devin returned to Tycho a couple months after she got back from the hospital. She walked this time, along the streets of mostly abandoned homes or wrecks torn to pieces by past storms. She was weak from her inpatient hospital stay and had yet to regain her running legs. The path was only visible by the patch of new growth in the aging woods and she followed it carefully, an eye out for snakes. When she reached the crater, it was mostly grown over, a flourish of plant life covering any sign that anyone had ever lived there.

Devin walked the perimeter of the crater, tried to find the path back to Trinity's magic beach, but the path was invisible now, only a memory which she couldn't follow because the memory was fading, fogging away. She thought about hallucinations, like maybe she made the whole thing up. Maybe she had created the world she wanted and brought it to life in this clearing as part of her mind's last battle for survival. But as she finished her lap of the crater, her toe caught on something buried in the dirt. She dug at it, the glint of metal sticking up in the sunlight that crept through the trees. When she unearthed the PBR can, there was no greater treasure. She held it up and chucked it skyward, toward outer space, where Tycho was mirrored in the faint daytime moon.

Devin started running soon after her final visit to Tycho, but she ran less and never looked for the path again.

She continues running into her early sixties. By this time, their house has weathered other hurricanes, not only Cherise, but Aramondo, Justinian. The engineer's house has not yet been lapped up by the ocean. Both of the children have moved off, Andrew to L.A. to work as an animator and Layla to New Orleans where she is sous chef at a restaurant in the French Quarter. It is only Devin and Ely and Fingerlickin dining in air conditioning, refusing to move inland no matter how many times the first floor floods as the hurricane waves beat at their door.

They are becoming typical middle-class Americans, which worries Devin but for their mutual honesty. The desire for a younger woman that Ely hid from Devin comes to light and their sex evolves into afternoon role-playing sessions where the living room becomes various settings, and they lie in bed breathing heavily afterward, giving each other notes on their performances. Also, Devin tells her husband when she needs to be alone. For Thanksgiving, he takes the flight to dreary Cincinnati for the last time before his parents pass away while Devin buys a cheap ticket to France and wanders a surprisingly unpeopled Louvre, listening to her own echoes. When they see each other back in Sunport, they both realize what a treasure it is to miss someone and see them once again.

Evenings, Devin runs through the town. There has been a mild resurgence of tourism and Sunport Beach is being rebuilt again. Again and again, a rebuilding, then a storm. Forgetting. Remembering. Refusing. Rebar skeletons skinned in cement, cranes lowering steel beams of high rises with private beach access. Even the Beach Bum dive bar jumps on board, garnishing drinks with pineapple instead of sickly-sweet cherries. Devin and Ely receive more offers from a firm representing Global Hyatt who wants to buy their land, demolish their house, and add on to a potential resort. The land is just far enough away from the ocean, and the world has put in just enough work to thwart global warming that a hotel there could last a few more years. But she and Ely are staying put.

Devin says, How much do you think they will go up? Half a million? A million?

Doesn't matter, says Ely. We can't let these capitalist bastards tell us what to do. This house has been ours for 33 years. It's an heirloom.

This is the first time Devin has noticed what the house really means to Ely, and though she doesn't mind moving wherever, anywhere, she is touched by the way he clings to legacy. She likes his tenacity.

Ely says, My uncle didn't weather Dominic in this old beaut just to let it rot. A captain who stayed with his ship only for his nephew to desert it? I'll tell you, we will never relinquish our land to the capitalists!

Ely is being extravagant and Devin can't hold her laughter. He leans into her on the couch, hugs her, puts his head on her shoulder, and she leans back into him. Devin says, You crazy old man.

When the next hurricane comes, they are forced to leave with everyone else.

Ely says, They're calling it Hurricane Trinity because it's really three storms all in one.

Trinity, says Devin, My god! What a coincidence.

But Ely is already heading through the door carrying two accent lamps. Devin tries to bring back Trinity's face, but can only picture an empty crater, a dazzling secret beach.

Outside, Layla coaches the movers who gather Devin and Ely's belongings into the truck. Layla will take Fingerlickin, since the hotel won't allow pets in the room. It has been raining for 24 hours and Beachfront Boulevard is completely invisible now, only dirty gray froth, winds battering the shore. The Weather Channel believes this storm will end the beach once and for all. The Global Hyatt tower under construction is already abandoned and wasted.

Devin and Ely watch Trinity make landfall on TV from their hotel room in Kentucky, just across the river from Cincy, as the water crosses what is left of Beachfront Boulevard and continues to climb. The weatherman gets hit in the face with a branch while he shouts over the wind and the branch blows on. The camera captures water as high as the first story of the Sandy Springs Apartments a mile inland from their house, and they imagine that their home on the beach must be only a roof peaking through the waves. If that. Ely says, She'll stand. Twenty bucks says the house will still be there. But Devin knows Trinity has swallowed it.

And how cheesy, Devin thinks, to say something like that. Trinity, the woman, the storm, swallowing everything she knows, altering her life once again. Devin realizes that despite Ely's love for the house, she wants the building to crumble, wants the ocean to eat it, anemones poking out of holes in the brick wall, triggerfish in the ductwork. It is nothing for a storm to leave a place ravaged. It is nothing for the world to tear everything down. She thinks of the map that Trinity drew in the sand, the way she erased herself from one spot, touched down in another, a new woman. She imagines that Trinity is on the moon now, wearing astronaut gear as she drifts from crater to crater. She holds a cigarette ripped straight from scripture, and she lights the cigarette now, cracks a beer, grabs Devin's hand, and pulls her along the path to her secret lunar beach.

They watch TV until the storm wears its way to unimaginable silence. The sun stabs through cracks in the curtains, reveals a husband and wife on their Motel 6 bed, an empty pizza box between them. Devin swings her body off the mattress to take her pills, brush her teeth, get ready for the day. It is cooler this far north, cloudless as of yet. Ely says, Hey, Hon. Come here. Quick.

She rounds the corner, toothbrush in her mouth to see a helicopter shot of the wreckage. It circles their old spot of beach, towers collapsed and washed away, the Villas rubbled and strewn, and in the middle of the disaster their house still stands like a middle finger. Ely says, That's twenty bucks.

Devin stops brushing to give him a look and Ely says, What? Aren't you proud of our little home?

But Devin has made up her mind. It is not their home anymore. She slips her wallet, stashed with cash, into the cell phone pocket of her leggings, and leaves her phone on the nightstand. She does her stretches, laces up her Asics, and as soon as the door shuts behind her, she kicks off into an unfamiliar world that is neither safe nor entirely damaging. She passes the Best Western, cuts away from the steady stream of highway rush, slows to jog by the skatepark, keeps going past the rental car, the storage units where their entire life is parked in a U-Haul behind an aluminum gate. And she continues on, turning to loop through the public park, down a muddy path through the woods. She is fearless now. She keeps running.

The End

ACKNOWLEDGEMENTS

Thanks to all my Mansfield friends and family for helping me kick off this writing journey. And to my BG buddies, thanks for helping me grow during those pandemic years of grad school. My Denham Springs people, I wouldn't be here without you all. And my DC writers, it's always a blast both writing and not writing with you. Cheers!

Thanks to my Portland people at Unsolicited Press for helping me bring the best version of this book into the world.

Many of my edits were made possible by the gifts of time I received from Vermont Studio Center and The Elizabeth George Foundation to whom I'm immensely grateful.

And Llalan, my bookstore lady, my patient first reader, my love. Thanks for all the rest.

ABOUT THE AUTHOR

Nick Rees Gardner has worked as a winemaker, chef, painter, shoe salesman, teacher, and addiction counselor. His fiction, nonfiction, and poetry have been published widely and his book of sonnets, *So Marvelously Far*, which tracks a life of substance abuse and recovery through a postindustrial Mansfield, Ohio, was published in 2019. Currently, he orders beer for a small wine and beer shop in the DC area and reviews books in his free time.

ABOUT UNSOLICITED PRESS

Unsolicited Press is based out of Portland, Oregon and focuses on the works of the unsung and underrepresented. As a womxn-owned, all-volunteer small publisher that doesn't worry about profits as much as championing exceptional literature, we have the privilege of partnering with authors skirting the fringes of the lit world. We've worked with emerging and award-winning authors such as Shann Ray, Amy Shimshon-Santo, Brook Bhagat, Kris Amos, and John W. Bateman.

Learn more at unsolicitedpress.com. Find us on twitter and instagram.

HURRICANE TRINITY

Copyright © 2023 Nick Rees Gardner

All Rights Reserved.

Published by Unsolicited Press.

Printed in the United States of America.

First Edition.

No part of this book may be used or reproduced in any manner whatsoever without written permission except in the case of brief quotations embodied in critical articles or reviews.

Attention schools and businesses: for discounted copies on large orders, please contact the publisher directly.

For information contact:

Unsolicited Press

Portland, Oregon

www.unsolicitedpress.com

orders@unsolicitedpress.com

619-354-8005

Front Cover Design: Kathryn Gerhardt

Editor: Jay Kristensen Jr.

ISBN: 978-1-956692-79-2

Printed in the USA
CPSIA information can be obtained
at www.ICGtesting.com
JSHW082137201223
53997JS00003B/165

9 781956 692792